pas [pa...]

glissade [glee-sad]

pas de chat [pa-duh-sha]

Ballewiena

Rebecca Bender

pajamapress

Dotty dreamed of being a ballet dancer.
When told to sit, she would *plié*.

When asked to stay,
she would *assemblé*.

When commanded to roll over, she would *pirouette*.

During a walk, her sisters
Jazzebelle and Miffy would
heel to Ms. Austere.
Dotty would practice
her dance moves.

She *chasséed* down the sidewalk,
stepped in *glissade* at the park,
and pranced in *pas de chat* by
the fire hydrant.

One day, she told herself,
she would perform for a real audience.

"SIT!"

"STAY!"

Unfortunately, Ms. Austere did not appreciate
Dotty's dancing. She was busy training Jazzebelle
and Miffy for their performance at the
GOLDEN BOW TALENT SHOW.
Sit and *stay* were not Dotty's specialty.

With a tug of her leash,
Ms. Austere led Dotty to
The Canine School of Obedience.

Obedience school was grueling.

"SIT."
Dotty moved
into a *passé*.

"SIT."
Dotty posed
in a *croisé*.

"SIT!"

Dotty tried, she really did, but something inside her made her spring up into an elegant *entrechat*.

It was no use. Dotty wasn't cut out to sit and stay and roll over. After class, she ran off in tears. "All I want to do is dance," she whimpered. "I'll never make it to the stage this way." Why did no one see her talent?

Eventually, her sobs were interrupted by a chattering voice.

"Cheer up, *Pitou*."

Dotty looked up to see a peculiar squirrel.

"My name is Louis-Pierre. I am a performer myself, although my specialty is acrobatics. Join me in my daily workout— you might learn a thing or two!"

Dotty didn't usually chase
squirrels, but she was intrigued.

Around and around
the park they went.

When the squirrel leaped,
Dotty leaped in *jeté*.

When he ran in a circle,
Dotty spun in *fouetté*.

When he balanced on one leg, Dotty held an *arabesque*.

"Pitou, I know just how to help you," said Louis-Pierre. "Meet me here tomorrow."

Dotty met Louis-Pierre every day after class.
His tutelage methods were most unusual.

Chase, but do not bite!

Roll, but do not shake!

Catch, but do not chew!

Dotty practiced and practiced, even when she wanted to give up.

Louis-Pierre encouraged her. "Look how much discipline you've gained, Pitou! The more focus you have, the better you dance."

Rehearsal was hard work. Dotty thought about Jazzebelle and Miffy. No wonder they practiced the same tricks over and over with Ms. Austere.

Then came the day of
THE GOLDEN BOW TALENT SHOW.
Ms. Austere brought Dotty along to watch
Jazzebelle and Miffy perform.

Dotty was miserable sitting in the audience. Her
toes twitched, and she *piquéed* from one paw
to another. She wanted to be on stage, but Ms.
Austere had her on a tight leash.

Then, just as her ears began to droop, Dotty felt a tickle by her collar.
"Pitou, this is your chance!"

Louis-Pierre was undoing her leash! Dotty's heart leaped in anticipation. Her friend did an aerial flip onto the curtain, and the hound on stage caught whiff of him.

A chase ensued. Around and around they went
until the squirrel led the hound out of sight.
"Show them what you've got, Pitou!" he called out.

"The show must go on," cried the producer.
"Who has an act ready to—?"

Before he'd finished his sentence, Dotty was
on the stage posing in first position.
Ms. Austere gasped.
Jazzebelle and Miffy gaped.

The producer made a quick decision and cued some graceful music.

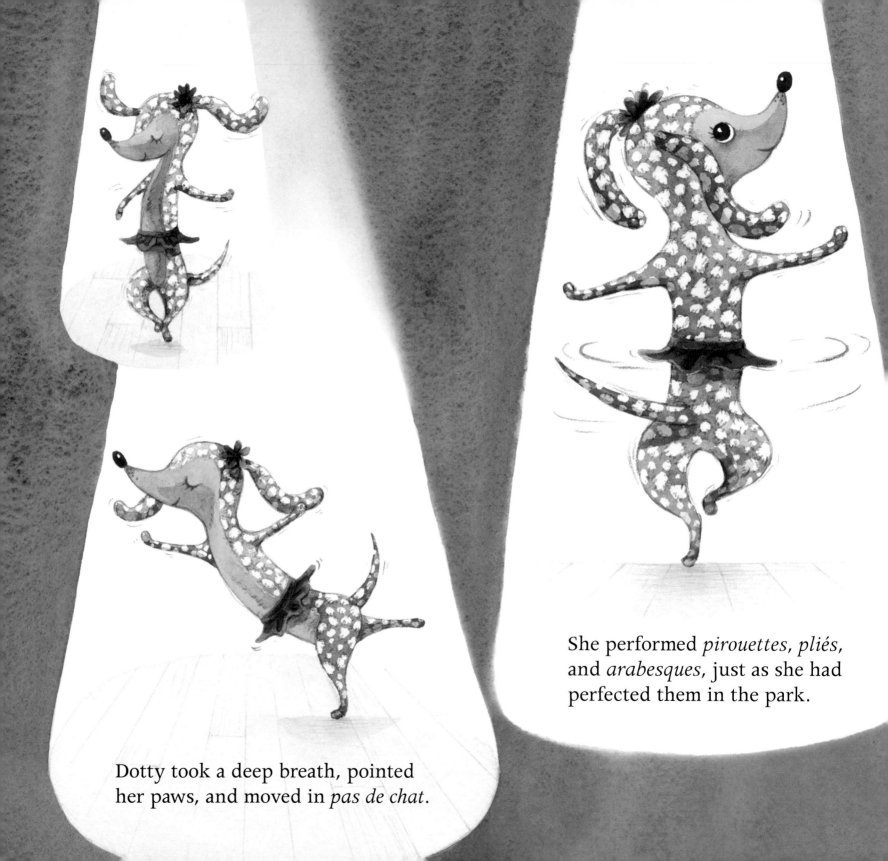

She performed *pirouettes*, *pliés*, and *arabesques*, just as she had perfected them in the park.

Dotty took a deep breath, pointed her paws, and moved in *pas de chat*.

For the finale, Dotty soared in a glorious *grand jeté* that left the crowd speechless.

Seconds later, thunderous applause broke out.
Dotty *chasséed* back into the spotlight for her *révérence*.

The audience whistled and howled.
Dotty bowed and curtsied.
Ms. Austere approached the stage.

"Dotty," she said, "I didn't realize you were a ballet dancer."

With Ms. Austere's blessing, Dotty transferred from the Canine School of Obedience to *l'Académie de ballet aux pitous*. There, she danced out her dreams.

Of course she continued to train with Louis-Pierre at the park. In time, she even learned to appreciate a good *sit* and *stay*.

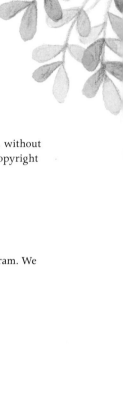

For Robyn

First published in Canada and the United States in 2022

Text and illustration copyright © 2022 Rebecca Bender
This edition copyright © 2022 Pajama Press Inc.
This is a first edition.

10 9 8 7 6 5 4 3 2 1

www.pajamapress.ca   info@pajamapress.ca

 Canada Council Conseil des arts
for the Arts du Canada
 ONTARIO ARTS COUNCIL
CONSEIL DES ARTS DE L'ONTARIO
an Ontario government agency
un organisme du gouvernement de l'Ontario
 Canadä

The publisher gratefully acknowledges the support of the Canada Council for the Arts and the Ontario Arts Council for its publishing program. We acknowledge the financial support of the Government of Canada through the Canada Book Fund (CBF) for our publishing activities.

Library and Archives Canada Cataloguing in Publication
Title: Ballewiena / Rebecca Bender.
Names: Bender, Rebecca, 1980- author, illustrator.
Identifiers: Canadiana 20200362402 | ISBN 9781772781373 (hardcover)
Classification: LCC PS8603.E5562 B35 2022 | DDC jC813/.6—dc23

Publisher Cataloging-in-Publication Data (U.S.)
Names: Bender, Rebecca, 1980-, author.
Title: Ballewiena / Rebecca Bender.
Description: Toronto, Ontario Canada: Pajama Press, 2022. | Summary: "Dotty the dachshund dreams of being a ballet dancer. Commanded to sit or stay, Dotty shows off her plié and assemblé instead. After a squirrel in the park helps Dotty discover how she can learn discipline her own way, she finally has the chance to perform on stage"— Provided by publisher.
Identifiers: ISBN 978–1–77278–137–3 (hardback)
Subjects: LCSH: Dachshunds -- Juvenile fiction. | Ballet -- Juvenile fiction. | Self-esteem – Juvenile fiction. | Humorous stories. | BISAC: JUVENILE FICTION / Performing Arts / Dance. | JUVENILE FICTION / Animals / Dogs. | JUVENILE FICTION / Social Themes / Self-Esteem & Self-Reliance.
Classification: LCC PZ7. B464Bal | DDC [E] – dc23

Original art created with gouache, watercolor, pencil, ink and digital media
Cover and book design—Rebecca Bender, Lorena González Guillén

Printed in China by WKT Company

Pajama Press Inc.
11 Davies Ave., Suite 103, Toronto, Ontario, Canada M4M 2A9

Distributed in Canada by UTP Distribution
5201 Dufferin Street Toronto, Ontario Canada, M3H 5T8

Distributed in the U.S. by Ingram Publisher Services
1 Ingram Blvd. La Vergne, TN 37086, USA

piqué [peek-ay]

jeté [jhet-ay]

grand jeté [gron-jhet-ay]

fouetté [foo-et-ay]

révérance